Ed Mouse

Finds Out About

Times of Day

Published by Raintree Steck-Vaughn Publishers, an imprint of Steck-Vaughn Company

Editor: Kathy DeVico
Project Manager: Joyce Spicer
Cover Design: Gino Coverty
Series Designer: Helen James
Illustrator: Adam Stower/Wildlife Art Agency
Consultants: Wendy Body, Chris Powling

Library of Congress Cataloging-in-Publication Data
Head, Honor.
Times of day/by Honor Head;
illustrated by Adam Stower.
p. cm.—(Ed mouse finds out about)
Summary: The concept of time is introduced as an adventurous mouse performs his daily activities. At various points in the text the reader is asked to answer questions based on the illustrations.
ISBN 0-8172-5203-7 (hardcover)
ISBN 0-8172-8103-7 (softcover)
[1. Time—Fiction. 2. Mice—Fiction.] I. Stower, Adam, ill. II. Title.
PZ7H335Ewt   1999
[E]—dc21   70743
97-32560
CIP
AC
Printed in Hong Kong
Bound in the United States
1 2 3 4 5 6 7 8 9 0 WO 02 01 00 99 98

Ed Mouse
Finds Out About
Times of Day

By Honor Head

Illustrated by
Adam Stower

RSVP
RAINTREE
STECK-VAUGHN
P U B L I S H E R S
A Steck-Vaughn Company

Austin, Texas

Meet Ed Mouse. He lives in a mousehole in a big house. Ed Mouse has lots of adventures. Why don't you join him?

Hi, there! I'm Ed.

5

Ed's alarm clock rings at 7 o'clock in the morning. Ed wakes up, yawns, and stretches. Today he is going skating with his friend Jo.

Do you like getting up in the mornings? What time do you get up?

7

What do you do in the morning? What do you like to eat for breakfast?

9

Ed finds his skates,
and they set off.
The sun is shining
and the sky is blue,
but it's a cold day.

Wait for me!

Come on, Ed!

Is it day or night when the sun shines? Is the sky blue at night?

11

By midmorning, they are hungry. Jo says it's too early for lunch, so they eat a snack. Then they build a snowmouse.

12

At 12 o'clock, noon, it's time for lunch. Ed and Jo find somewhere dry to have their picnic and unpack their sandwiches.

Yummy! Cheese and tomato.

15

After lunch Ed and Jo
pack up their picnic
things. Then they put
on their skates and race
across the pond. A duck
on the bank is taking
an afternoon nap.

You can't catch me!

What do you do after lunch? Do you take an afternoon nap?

17

Suddenly, Ed and Jo notice that it's getting late. The afternoon is darker and colder. It's time to go home. Ed looks at the map to find a shortcut.

How can you tell it is getting late? Why does it get dark?

18

19

They walk and walk through the snow. By the time it is evening, they are lost. Jo looks at the map. Ed was reading it upside-down!

20

21

Jo thinks she can find the way home. Now it is very dark, and the moon is out.
Ed is hungry. He has missed dinnertime.

Almost there!

22

What can you see in the sky?
How is the sky at night
different from during the day?

At last they reach home. It's very late. Jo says good night to Ed. She's tired and hungry. Ed's too sleepy to eat dinner.

Good night, Ed.

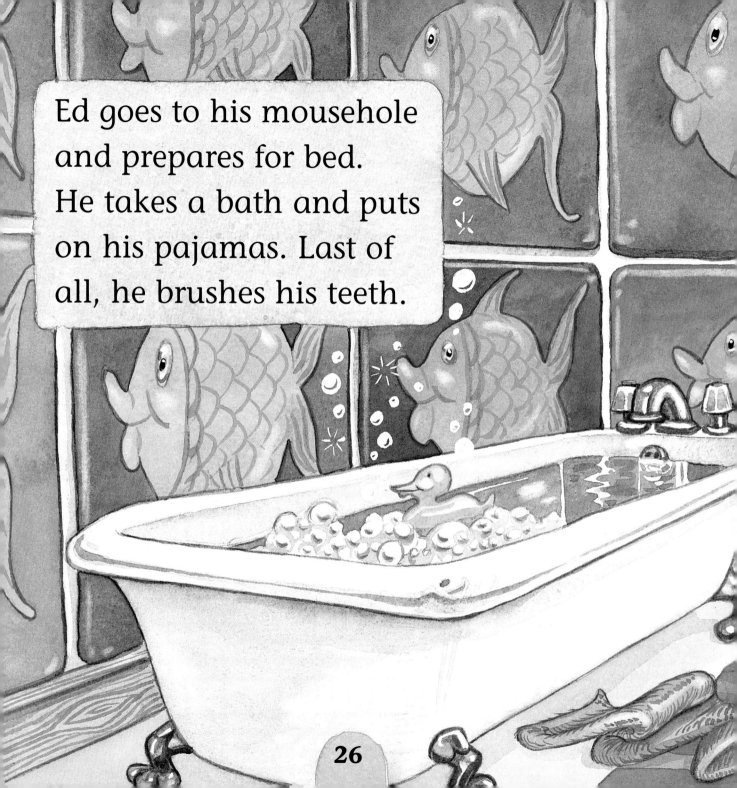

Ed goes to his mousehole and prepares for bed. He takes a bath and puts on his pajamas. Last of all, he brushes his teeth.

Snuggled up in bed Ed reads his favorite book, turns out the light, and falls asleep. Ed dreams he is a famous skier, whizzing down snowy slopes. Good night, Ed.

What is your favorite bedtime story? What do you dream about while you sleep?

Notes for Parents and Teachers

This book is about different times of day. Read the book through so that the children become familiar with the story and with the characters. Point out the speech bubbles, and make sure the children understand that these indicate someone is talking. Once the children are familiar with the story, read it through again, and ask them to answer the questions. Ask the children to describe what happens in the story, using as many words that describe times of day as they can.

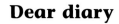

Dear diary

Ask the children to draw a picture diary. Ask them to draw what they do throughout the day, then talk about what they have drawn. Encourage the children to think about the different things they do during the morning, afternoon, evening, and night.

Mealtimes

Ask the children to describe their favorite breakfast, lunch, and evening meals. Encourage them to find magazine and newspaper pictures of their favorite foods, and to talk about their favorite snacks. Then ask them to think about foods they don't like and why they don't like them.

Storytime

Ask the children to make up a story about something that happens during the night and something that happens during the day. Encourage them to use as many nighttime and daytime words as possible.

What to wear

Gather different types of clothes—shoes, hats, gloves, and so on. Divide the children into groups, representing a summer day, a winter day, a summer night, and a winter night. Ask each group to choose the clothes they would wear. When they have finished, discuss the choices they have made. Compare the daytime and nighttime clothes with the winter and summer clothes.

Make a mobile

Using cardboard, ask the children to draw several things they might see in the sky at night or during the day, such as the sun, moon, a rainbow, fluffy white clouds, stars, and so on. Cut out some of the shapes, and make a daytime mobile and a nighttime mobile.

31

List of Words

A duck is taking an **afternoon** nap.

Ed takes a **bath**.

It is **bedtime**.

Ed has **breakfast**.

It is getting **dark**.

Ed **dreams**.

Ed gets **dressed**.

It is **evening**.

Good night, Ed.

Time for **lunch**.

At **midmorning** Ed and Jo have a snack.

The **moon** is out.

Ed's alarm clock rings in the **morning**.

It is **noon**.

Ed puts on his **pajamas**.

Ed **stretches**.

The **sun** is shining.

Ed **wakes up**.

Ed **yawns**.